THE CASE WITH NO CLUES

NO CLUES

LEILA & NUGGET MYSTERY #2

D1113783

DESERAE & DUSTIN BRADY

CONTENTS

OTHER BOOKS
BY DUSTIN BRADY

ACKNOWLEDGMENTS

Special thanks to April Brady for the cover and interior illustrations. You can follow April's artwork on Instagram: @aprilynnart.

BURIED TREASURE

"Thanks, Miss Carol!" Leila said to the bus driver as she jumped the last step out of the bus and ran toward her house.

"Wait up!" Leila's friend Kait yelled.

Leila sighed and slowed down.

"Want to do something fun?" Kait asked when she caught up.

"Sorry, can't," Leila answered, still on the move.

Kait continued as if she hadn't heard Leila. "I think I can make my brother play with us today. If not, I have an idea for a new way to spy on my sister. Or, hey, did I tell you about that five-pound gummy bear I saw online? Maybe we could…"

"I'm really sorry," Leila replied, speeding up again.

"Come on!" Kait struggled to keep up. "Whatever it is can't be that important."

Oh, it was definitely that important. Leila had been counting down the minutes to this moment ever since math class had ended at 10:30. That was five hours ago, and five hours is a really long time to count down to anything. Her elderly neighbor, Mrs. Crenshaw, had promised to tell her about a super-old mystery and hidden treasure this afternoon. A hidden treasure! Just like the movies! Leila got butterflies in her tummy every time she thought about it. "See you tomorrow!" Leila yelled over her shoulder as she ran up her driveway.

Inside the house, she hugged her mom, hugged her little dog Nugget and said the five magic words: "Wanna go for a walk?" Nugget leaped high enough to touch Leila's nose with his own. Leila smiled, clipped on the leash and ran the whole way to Mrs. Crenshaw's house.

Mrs. Crenshaw had opened the door before Leila got to the porch. "Come in, Miss Detective! I've been waiting for you."

Nugget looked up and wagged his tail, hoping for a treat. Mrs. Crenshaw pulled a dog biscuit out of her pocket. "Yes, I've been waiting for you too," she said. Nugget wagged his tail harder and stood on his back legs as Mrs. Crenshaw flipped him the treat.

Before Nugget could even swallow the biscuit, Leila had sat at the kitchen table and opened her detective notebook to the unsolved case. "I'm ready!"

"I have cookies in the oven," Mrs. Crenshaw said. "Don't you want to wait until they're ready?"

"Nooooooooo!" Leila pretended to melt in her seat. "You've got to tell me now! I've been dying ever since we talked yesterday!"

Mrs. Crenshaw laughed. "OK, OK," she said. "I suppose I owe you." Mrs. Crenshaw grabbed an old school yearbook from the counter and flipped through it until she landed on a black-and-white picture of a man with thick glasses, a thin mustache and a gleam in his eye. "Do you know who this is?"

Leila shook her head.

"This is Mr. McGee. He was the first principal at Englewood Elementary School."

"That's where I go to school!" Leila exclaimed.

Mrs. Crenshaw smiled and nodded. "I went there too," she said. "Look." She flipped a few pages and pointed to a girl with tight curls and a smile that was

5

almost too big for her face. "That little girl was never more excited for anything in her life than she was for June 4, 1947 — the last day of third grade. That was the day of the treasure hunt."

Leila scooted forward in her chair. Finally, the good stuff.

Mrs. Crenshaw continued. "Mr. McGee was the best principal. There were more than 400 kids in school, and Mr. McGee had nicknames for every single one of them. I was Nance, after Nancy Drew, because I was so good at solving mysteries. Mr. McGee loved mysteries, and he loved surprises. He loved them so much that a few weeks before my third-grade year ended, he announced that he'd have a special mystery for the whole school to solve together on the last day of school. It would be a treasure hunt, and the student who found the treasure first got to keep it."

"What was the treasure?"

"Mr. McGee wouldn't tell anyone," Mrs. Crenshaw said. "It was probably just some little trinket, but people started saying that they'd heard Mr. McGee had buried a treasure chest under the playground or he'd inherited a bunch of gold coins or he secretly owned a toy store. One boy was even going around school telling everybody that Principal McGee used to be a pirate."

Leila wrote, "Pirate?" in her notes and looked back up.

Mrs. Crenshaw continued. "On the last day, everyone was buzzing. A lot of kids brought magnifying glasses or dressed up as Sherlock Holmes. The pirate boy wore a patch. We all gathered at the flagpole for our first clue. We waited and waited, but Mr. McGee never showed up. One of the teachers finally got word that his wife had gotten sick, and Mr. McGee had gone to the hospital with her in the middle of the night. The treasure hunt was canceled."

"That stinks," Leila said. "But you were able to do the treasure hunt the next year, right?"

Mrs. Crenshaw shook her head. "Mrs. McGee's health got worse. They moved across the country that summer so she could get better care."

Leila was starting to understand. "So the treasure stayed hidden."

"Everyone else forgot about it, but I couldn't," Mrs. Crenshaw said. "I looked all over the school for clues. I thought that if I could just find one, I'd be able to pick up the trail and solve the mystery. I stayed an hour after school for a month straight, searching classrooms, questioning teachers and reading about famous treasure hunts. I even started digging in the corner of the playground before the janitor noticed and made me stop."

"But you never found it?"

"Nobody's found it."

"And you think I can find it? After 70 years? With no clues or anything?!" This wasn't exactly the news Leila had been hoping for.

"I know it probably won't happen," Mrs. Crenshaw said. "After 70 years, the clues are almost definitely gone by now. I just remember how much fun I had treasure hunting, and I thought you'd enjoy it too. Plus, it's going to be gone for good in a few months."

Leila nodded. After 78 years, Englewood Elementary was finally getting a new building. When Leila's bus passed the construction site for the new school every morning, she always strained to catch a glimpse of the progress on its gigantic playground. By June, the current school building would be nothing but a memory.

Leila sighed. "OK," she said. "I'll take the case. It doesn't hurt to look, right?"

Even though Leila was reluctant to start, the mystery soon sucked her in. Mrs. Crenshaw was right — treasure hunting was a lot of fun. Before Leila knew it, she was memorizing every half-clue and maybe-clue Mrs. Crenshaw had written down as a kid. She secretly scoured every dusty corner and tall cabinet in the school for anything that looked old. She talked to Nugget so much about the case that even he seemed to get tired of it.

After a few weeks of no clues, though, Leila's interest in the treasure started to fizzle. Sure, she wanted to find it, but she had to face the facts — the trail was gone. Other cases started to crowd the treasure out of her mind. Every day, the new building was looking more like a school, and every day, Leila cared less that the old building and its treasure were going to be gone soon. After two months, Leila had all but forgotten about treasure hunt mystery.

That all changed the day she found clue number one.

2

CLUE NUMBER ONE

Leila wasn't even trying to find the hidden treasure the day she stumbled upon the first clue. She was working on a completely different mystery that morning — the Case of How to Stay Awake During the World's Most Boring History Lesson.

"And this is Millard Fillmore," Leila's teacher, Mrs. Pierce, said as she changed the picture on the screen. "He was the thirteenth president. He installed the first bathtub in the White House. Here's a picture of that bathtub."

Mrs. Pierce could make any lesson exciting — especially history — but even she was struggling with the "Presidents You've Never Heard Of" chapter. "And this is Grover Cleveland. He actually served two different terms in the White House. Can you imagine being president two different times?"

Yup. Leila could imagine it pretty easily. Her eyelids started drooping, so she concentrated on the picture of Grover Cleveland to stay awake. She stared at his bushy mustache and bowtie. She wondered what it would be like to have the name, "Grover." Wait, was this the guy who invented Cleveland? Her eyelids were getting heavy again.

Then, Mrs. Pierce changed the picture again, and Leila gasped out loud.

"This is William Henry Harrison," Mrs. Pierce said. "He was president for the shortest amount of time — only 31 days."

Leila's hand shot up.

"Yes, Leila!" Mrs. Pierce said, beaming. She seemed happy that at least one person in the class was paying close enough attention that they would have a question.

"Did William Henry Harrison have

anything to do with our school?" Leila asked.

Mrs. Pierce looked confused. "Well, he died long before our school was built, and I don't think he ever visited our town. Why do you ask?"

"No reason!" Leila said, her face turning red. "Silly question!"

But it wasn't a silly question. Leila had seen the face somewhere before, and she was almost positive she'd seen it at the school. But where? It took her another two minutes to figure it out, and when she did, she gasped again. The girl in front of her turned around to give her a dirty look. "Sorry," Leila mouthed.

With the building closing for good at the end of the school year, the principal had decided to dig up a bunch of old stuff from Englewood Elementary's history and display it in the hallways.

Leila had spent hours studying the pictures and knick-knacks because she knew they were probably her only chance of finding the clues that Mr. McGee had hidden all those years ago.

One of the things she'd studied for a whole week was the staff picture collection. Every year, the school displayed a group picture of all of the school's teachers in the hallway next to the office. Leila was never sure why the school did that — maybe so students wouldn't forget what their teacher looked like? This year the school had lined an entire hallway with staff pictures going back to the 1940s. Leila spent the longest time staring at the 1947 picture to learn whatever she could about the year of the treasure hunt. Turns out, Mr. McGee had hidden a very important clue in the picture.

The moment school let out, Leila ran for the picture. She had to see if she was right. When she got there, she caught her breath. In the second row of the picture, surrounded by 120 serious teachers, was the face of a man who'd died 100 years before the picture was even taken. It was President William Henry Harrison.

3

HALL OF PRESIDENTS

When Kait sat next to Leila on the bus, she gave her friend a weird look.

"You OK?" Kait asked.

"Uh, yeah! Of course!" Leila said.

"Cuz you're doing that face that people make on Scooby-Doo when they've seen a ghost."

"Oh! Haha! Weird!" Leila said. She wanted so much to tell someone about her discovery, but she knew that if she told Kait, the whole school would know in about two seconds, and she needed to keep this secret a little longer — at least until she could ask Mrs. Crenshaw about it.

Kait frowned at Leila like she didn't believe her, but she decided to drop it. The two girls went their separate ways off the bus. Leila walked to her house like everything was normal, but as soon as she stepped inside, she started running.

Her mom tilted her head after Leila gave her the world's fastest hug. "What's got you so excited?" she asked.

"I just found a big clue in a case!" Leila said, fumbling with Nugget's leash. "A BIG clue! I've got to tell Mrs. Crenshaw!"

"OK," Leila's mom said. "Just make sure you're home in time for dinner."

"Of course!" Leila shouted, already two steps out the door. Nugget matched her step-for-step as she raced to Mrs. Crenshaw's house. When she reached the front door, she started knocking and knocking.

Mrs. Crenshaw came to the door, annoyed. "What?" she asked harshly before looking down to see Leila and Nugget.

"The first clue!" Leila gasped. "I found the first clue!"

Mrs. Crenshaw's face softened, and she opened the door. "The first clue to what, dear? That missing stuffed animal you've been helping your friend find?"

"THE TREASURE!" Leila squealed, skipping into the house.

Mrs. Crenshaw's eyes got wide. Nugget bounded around the room in glee — not that he knew what was going on, but everyone was so excited that he had to bound. After a full minute, both Leila and Nugget calmed down enough that Leila could finally tell Mrs. Crenshaw the whole story of her discovery. "Can you believe it?!" Leila asked when she'd finally finished.

Mrs. Crenshaw folded her arms across her chest. She looked like she wanted to believe it, but she wasn't convinced yet. "Are you sure it was President Harrison?" Mrs. Crenshaw asked. "It's a blurry, old picture, and a lot of blurry, old pictures look the same."

"Very sure!" Leila exclaimed. "Surer than sure! If you look really close at the picture, you can see where Principal McGee cut around the president's head and glued it on there. But what could it mean?!"

"The Hall of Presidents," Mrs. Crenshaw said.

"What's that?"

"Principal McGee was very big on history, so he lined the whole east hallway of the school with pictures and facts about U.S. presidents — from

Washington all the way to Truman. This clue must be saying that the next clue is hidden behind Harrison's picture."

Leila's shoulders slumped. "But that picture isn't there anymore."

"Right."

"Oh."

"I'm sorry, honey. But that was an excellent job finding the first clue! In 70 years, you're the only person who's ever noticed it."

Leila was too deep in thought to take the compliment. "But what if the clue's still there?"

Mrs. Crenshaw shook her head. "That picture of Harrison is long gone. Nobody's keeping a poster that old."

"But what if the clue wasn't on the poster? What if it was somewhere nearby?"

Mrs. Crenshaw shrugged. "Even so,

it's not going to last 70 years."

"This clue did!" Leila was warming up to this idea. "Do you remember where Harrison would have been in the hallway?"

"I could figure it out, but…"

"Please? Oh please, could you show me?!"

Even though Mrs. Crenshaw was shaking her head, a tiny sliver of her mouth had turned up into a smile, giving her away.

Leila saw that sliver and knew that Mrs. Crenshaw wanted to find this treasure just as much as she did. "Pleeeeeeeeease?"

Mrs. Crenshaw huffed. "My nephew's the school janitor. I suppose I could give him a call."

"Yay!" Leila danced around the room. "Nugget, we're going for a ride!" Nugget danced too.

Mrs. Crenshaw called her nephew, Leila called her mom, and five minutes later, they were ready to leave. Mrs. Crenshaw eyed Nugget as she unlocked her car. "He's not going to shed all over my seats, is he?"

"Oh no!" Leila exclaimed. "He's a cavapoo!"

"A what?" Mrs. Crenshaw asked with squinty eyes.

"Cavapoo! That means he's part poodle, so he doesn't shed!"

Nugget looked up and wagged his tail proudly.

Mrs. Crenshaw thought about it for another few seconds, then sighed. "I've never let a dog in my car before. He'd better watch himself."

"He will! I'll make sure of it!" Leila scooped Nugget into her arms and sat on the spotless back seat of Mrs. Crenshaw's car.

Three minutes later, they arrived at the school. "OK, Nugget, you be good in here," Leila said as she left the dog in the car. "We'll just be gone for a few minutes."

Nugget scrambled to the door and watched Mrs. Crenshaw and Leila walk away. He pressed his nose to the window, fogging it all up. Mrs. Crenshaw turned and shook her head at Nugget. He stared back at her, wagging his tail and fogging the window more.

"Is he going to keep doing that?" Mrs. Crenshaw asked.

"Oh yeah," Leila said. "He's going to stay right there until we come back."

Mrs. Crenshaw rolled her eyes and walked back to the car. "We'd better bring him with us then," she said.

Leila's eyes got big. "You mean it's OK to take a dog into the school?"

"It's going to have to be OK," Mrs. Crenshaw said. "I don't want him snotting all over my windows."

Leila opened the door, and Nugget leaped out, overjoyed that he got to join the adventure.

"Keep him on a leash and let me do any talking," Mrs. Crenshaw said.

The janitor, Mr. Peterman, was taking down the flag for the day when Leila, Nugget and Mrs. Crenshaw walked up. He looked down at Nugget. "Oh no, Aunt Margaret! You didn't tell me…"

"It'll be fine, Daniel," she said. "The dog's housetrained, and he's a something-poo that doesn't shed."

"Cavapoo," Leila added helpfully.

Mrs. Crenshaw didn't wait for permission from the stunned Mr.

Peterman - she just took the key out of his hand and unlocked the school door. Leila hurried to join her as she started walking down a long hallway. "Harrison was the ninth president, so his picture would be nine doors down on the left," Mrs. Crenshaw said. Leila counted off the doors until they got to the music room. The three of them stared at a bulletin board decorated with smiling musical notes.

"Well, this is it," Mrs. Crenshaw finally said.

"OK, so maybe the clue is underneath the decorations on the board," Leila suggested.

"It's not," Mrs. Crenshaw said. "This bulletin board wasn't even here when I was in school."

"So maybe it's on the wall behind the bulletin board!"

"For one thing, no. It's not. For another, I didn't bring my power tools to remove a bulletin board. Did you?"

Leila wasn't about to give up after coming all this way. "Well, maybe it's in the room behind the wall!"

Mrs. Crenshaw sighed. "We can check."

Leila, Nugget and Mrs. Crenshaw spent the next half hour searching the music room. Nugget found lots of crumbs to gobble up, but that was about it. Finally, Leila sighed. "I guess it's not in here," she said. "I'm sorry Mrs. Crenshaw. You were right. I guess I just really wanted to find that clue."

"It's OK, dear," Mrs. Crenshaw said. "I did too." They walked out to the hallway and stared at the bulletin board one last time. Nugget, who was still in crumb-finding mode, put his nose to the ground and started sniffing. He sniffed closer and closer to the wall. Then, he suddenly started sniffing like crazy and pawing at one of the bricks.

"Nugget!" Leila said. "Don't be bad! There's nothing…" She stopped in the middle of her sentence and got real close to the brick. A thin line had been cut into the wall all the way around the brick. She tried pushing on the brick. Nothing happened. She pushed harder. Still nothing. Nugget was staring at the brick with his eyes squinted and tail wagging. Leila sat on the ground, scooched Nugget out of the way and kicked the brick as hard as she could.

CRACK!

It broke free, revealing a small hole in the wall. Inside the hole was a package.

THE OCEAN BLUE

Nugget stopped dead in his tracks. Leila carefully pulled the package out of the wall and unwrapped it. Inside were a dozen 70-year-old chocolate bars. Leila picked up one of the bars and turned it over in her hand. The wrapper said "Bobo Bar! Fresh and Delicious!"

Mrs. Crenshaw's face lit up. "A Bobo Bar!" she said. "I haven't seen one of those for 50 years!"

"What is it?"

"They were supposed to be the freshest chocolate bars because they used a red, see-through inside wrapper instead of the usual silver paper. I don't think the red wrapper did anything special to keep the chocolate fresh, but it made me believe Bobo Bars were the best, so they always seemed to taste a little better."

"I don't think it's fresh anymore," Leila said, noticing the expiration date was September, 1949.

"Try opening it," Mrs. Crenshaw said. "Maybe there's a clue inside."

Leila made a face.

"Go ahead," Mrs. Crenshaw said. "It's just chocolate. It's not going to stink."

Leila held her nose just in case and carefully unpeeled the outside wrapper. Nothing but red plastic and an old candy bar inside. "I don't get it," Leila said. "Does this mean…" Leila stopped in the middle of her sentence when she took a second glance at the outside wrapper. There was writing underneath. Leila's eyes got huge as she read the message.

Good job by you,
You've found clue number two!
Here's a treat
For you to eat
As you solve the mystery.
In 1492,

Columbus sailed the ocean BLUE.
But what would it mean
If the sea were GREEN?
Would it really change the things you've READ?

Leila turned to Mrs. Crenshaw with the biggest grin on her face. "It's a clue! A real clue to a real treasure hunt! Eeee!"

Mrs. Crenshaw couldn't contain a little smile of her own. "Let's put the rest of these candy bars back into the wall and get out of here before my nephew sics the dog catcher on us.

Mrs. Crenshaw drove Leila home, and the two of them stayed in the car for 30 extra minutes trying to figure out the riddle. That night, Leila took twice as long as usual to finish her homework because her mind kept going back to the poem. On top of all her excitement about the clue, there was a little nervousness that she wouldn't figure it out in time. After all, there were only a few short months left in the school year.

The next day at school, Leila tried to concentrate. She really did. But no matter how hard she tried, she couldn't focus on the War of 1812 when all she wanted the teacher to talk about was Christopher Columbus. Things didn't get any better at lunch.

"...afraid of the tree?"

Leila looked over. Kait was staring at her like she was expecting an answer to a question. "What did you say?" Leila asked.

Kait huffed. "Why was the cat afraid of the tree?" she repeated.

Leila gave her a weird look. "Why would you ask me that?"

"It's the riddle on my Laffy Taffy!" Kait held up an empty wrapper. "I ask you my Laffy Taffy riddle every day! What's wrong with you?"

"I'm sorry," Leila said. "I've just had a lot on my mind lately."

"It's like I'm talking to a zombie,"

Kait said. She tapped Leila on the head a few times. "You're not a zombie, are you?"

"Don't be a weirdo," Leila said. Zombie. Was that a clue? Zombies are green, right?

"You sure there's nothing you want to tell me, Ms. Zombie?" Kait asked.

"Uh, no." Leila felt bad about fibbing to her friend, but she'd just come up with an idea. She needed to visit the library.

Kait looked at her with squinty eyes for a second, then said, "Because of its bark."

"Huh?"

"Because of its bark. That's the answer to the riddle."

Leila still looked confused. "Oh."

Kait threw her head back and yelled her frustration to the ceiling. "Unnnnnng!"

Leila looked at the clock and stood up. "Sorry, Kait. I've got to do something real quick."

"Probably eat some brains, right?!" Kait shouted after her. "Nice, juicy brains!"

Leila shook her head as she walked out the door. She just needed a few minutes to check out every Christopher Columbus book the school library had. Leila was convinced there was something she needed to learn about him to solve the riddle. At the library, she was disappointed to find that there was only one book about Christopher Columbus, and it was a thin one for little kids. "I'm sorry," the librarian said. "We just don't have many books like that anymore. Have you tried the Internet?"

Leila sighed, nodded and thanked the librarian. Then the bell rang, and she hurried to art class. Between the library and the art classroom was the music room. Leila's heart pounded faster as she neared it. The music room would always be her own secret spot — the place where she…

Leila suddenly stopped breathing and stopped walking. She put on the brakes so fast that the person walking behind her bumped into her back. The brick was gone, and the hiding spot was wide open. Leila ran over and bent down to look inside.

It was empty.

5

BOBO BARS

Leila started panicking. Who could have found the spot so fast? She didn't remember seeing another person in the whole school yesterday afternoon. Had someone been watching her? Wait, was someone watching now?! Leila popped her head up and looked at everyone walking by. Amelia? Did Amelia just give her a weird look? Why was Chase digging in his bookbag like that? What was he trying to hide? Leila spent the rest of the day trying to figure out who'd discovered her secret.

After school, Leila clipped the leash onto Nugget and loudly announced, "I'm going for a walk with the dog! Nothing special!" You know, just in case someone had put spy cameras into her house. Can't be too careful. Leila took 20 minutes to walk to Mrs. Crenshaw's house, zigging and zagging and spinning in circles the whole way. Nugget, of course, loved it. When she was sure that nobody had followed her, Leila walked up the driveway to her friend Javy Martinez's house, then cut through his backyard into Mrs. Crenshaw's yard. She snuck to her back door and knocked while looking over her shoulder.

Mrs. Crenshaw seemed surprised to see Leila at the wrong door. "What are you…" she started to ask before Leila ducked underneath her arm into the house. Mrs. Crenshaw closed the door and turned around with her arms crossed. "What's going on?" she asked.

Leila had wide eyes. When she opened her mouth, a bunch of words spilled out in a jumble. "A spy! There's a spy, and he's following me, and I don't know where he's at, and I don't know if he put cameras in my house, or…" At that moment, Leila's eyes got even bigger, which seemed impossible because they were already really wide, "...or your house! We need to look for cameras right now! They could be listening to us!" Leila started looking all around the ceiling like a crazy person.

Mrs. Crenshaw snapped her fingers in Leila's face. "Hey! Hey!" That got Leila's attention. "Stop talking nonsense. There are no cameras."

"But, but..." Leila was almost in tears by now. "But someone else found the second clue!"

"And?" Mrs. Crenshaw asked.

"And, well, isn't that bad?"

"No, it's not bad, and it certainly doesn't mean there's a spy," Mrs. Crenshaw said. "This isn't the movies. There aren't spies hiding cameras to win an elementary school scavenger hunt. As a detective, you've got to learn that the simplest answers are usually the right ones. Now, what's the simplest answer?"

"That someone hid a camera and…"

"Wrong," Mrs. Crenshaw interrupted. "The simplest answer is that my nephew saw you digging in the wall yesterday and took the weird bag of old candy bars to the office."

"Oh," Leila said, suddenly feeling a little silly. "I guess that makes sense."

"And even if another student happened to find the clue, so what? This is a treasure hunt! Treasure hunts are supposed to have competition."

Leila sure didn't want any competition, but if Mrs. Crenshaw was right, then she was still the only one who'd seen the clue. She started to feel better.

That is, until lunch the next day.

"Oh brother," Kait said, shaking her

head at her Laffy Taffy. "This is a grandpa joke."

"A grandpa joke?" Leila asked, her mouth full of apple.

"Yeah, a joke my grandpa would tell me when I was little. It's that old. Don't they pay someone there to write jokes? That's the job I want when I get older."

"Well, what is it?" Leila asked.

"What's black and white and red all over?" Kait read, rolling her eyes. "So lame."

"Black and white and red?" Leila hadn't heard that one before. "Wait don't tell me. I can figure it out."

"Sooooooo lame," Kait repeated.

"Is it like a zebra with…" Leila stopped in the middle of her answer because something across the cafeteria caught her attention. It was an older boy stuffing his face with a chocolate bar.

Next to his hands, crumpled in a ball was the unmistakable, clear red wrapper of a Bobo Bar.

Leila immediately stood up and started marching across the cafeteria. She'd found her spy, and she had a LOT of questions to ask him. The boy was much bigger than her, and she didn't know exactly what she'd say, but she wasn't about to let him get away with this. "Excuse me," she said when she arrived.

All the eyes at the table turned to Leila. "Uh, can I help you?" the boy asked.

Leila held out her finger like a lawyer pointing at the bad guy in court. "Where did you get that?"

The boy looked confused. "This? Did she try to sell you one too?"

Now it was Leila's turn to be confused. "Did who try to sell me one?"

"It's actually pretty gross," the kid said. "She acted like it was some rare candy that was going to be the best thing I'd ever tasted, so I gave her two dollars for it. Two whole dollars for a single candy bar! That was dumb. Don't let her trick you too."

"Let who trick me?" Leila asked. "Who sold that to you?"

The boy scanned the cafeteria, then finally found the candy dealer. "There," he said.

Leila spun around. He was pointing at Kait.

6
NEWSPAPER

When Leila made it back to the table, Kait was ready for her. "So you figured it out, huh detective?"

"Why would you spy on your best friend?" Leila asked.

"Why would you hide something from your best friend?" Kait shot back.

"I wasn't hiding it from you. I just wasn't telling you."

Kait blinked a few times. "That literally makes no sense."

Leila sighed. "How did you do it?"

Kait smiled a smug, little smile. "Well, you were clearly up to something the other day, so I got on my bike and followed you to that old lady's house."

"You know her name is Mrs. Crenshaw."

"Right, OK. So anyways, I waited outside for a few minutes, then just as I was about to give up and go back home, you guys got in the car. It looked like you were heading toward the school, so I biked there. When I finally got to the school, the janitor wouldn't let me in, but he told me that you went to the music room. The next day, I found the weird brick outside the music room, pulled it back and voila." Kait made a fancy motion with her hand and bowed.

"So you decided to sell the candy bars?"

"No," Kait said. "I decided to eat them. To get back at you. But they were gross, so then I decided to sell them."

"They were 70 years old," Leila said.

Kait made a face and turned a little green. "I did not know that."

"So you didn't care about the treasure?" Leila asked.

Kait looked at Leila out of the corner of her eye. "What treasure?"

"Do you have any of the candy bars with you now?" Leila asked.

Kait dug one out of her backpack. Leila peeled back the outside wrapper and showed her the riddle. Kait gasped. "What does that mean?!"

Leila told Kait everything about Principal McGee, the 70-year-old treasure and the president in the picture. It felt great to finally share things with her best friend again.

By the time she finished, Kait was exploding with questions. "So there's a buried treasure right here in the school?!"

Leila shrugged. "Probably."

"And nobody knows what it is?!"

"Nope."

"So it could be gold or something?!"

"I mean, probably not."

"Yeah. It's a treasure. It's definitely gold. And you didn't tell me about this gold — why, again?"

Leila sighed. "Because you have a tough time keeping secrets, and I didn't want the whole school to know about it."

Kait gasped and made a face like Leila had just hit her. "You wanted the treasure for yourself!"

"That's not it at all!" Leila said. "I was going to tell you! I mean, I just didn't think you could…"

"I wouldn't have told anyone," Kait said. "You know why? Because you're my friend. And friends keep secrets for each other. But I guess that's not as important to you as some dumb treasure." With that, Kait got up and stomped away, leaving her lunch behind.

"Kait! Come on, Kait!" Leila shouted after her friend. She started picking up Kait's stuff to take back to her. Was Kait right? Should Leila have shared her secret earlier? Leila was deep in thought when she picked up Kait's Laffy Taffy wrapper and noticed the answer to the joke Kait had been trying to tell her earlier. "A newspaper."

A newspaper? Even though Leila had a thousand things on her mind, the answer made her stop. That didn't make sense. Newspapers are black and white, but they sure aren't red. Leila turned the wrapper over and read the joke for herself. "What's black and white and read all over." Ohhhhh, now Leila understood. A newspaper is READ all over the place; it's not the color red. Funny. Well, not really funny, but funny in a grandpa joke kind of way. She crumpled the garbage and then cleaned the rest of Kait's mess. But as she was putting the Bobo Bar back into Kait's backpack, the candy bar's clear, red inside wrapper caught her eye. Leila held the Bobo Bar to her face.

"Of course! That's it!" she said to herself.

"Did you figure out the candy bar clue?" someone asked.

Leila's head shot up. Gwyneth Watson from Mrs. Liggins's third-grade class was sitting at the next table, holding up her own Bobo Bar. "We've been trying to figure it out all lunch," Gwyneth said. "What do you think it means?"

Leila's heart started pounding. How many people were now looking for the treasure? She had to find Kait.

7

RUNNING SHOES

Leila ran into Kait pacing angrily in the hallway. "Kait!" she said as she handed over the bookbag. "How many of those candy bars did you sell? I think I figured it out, but we need to hurry because…" Kait pretended that she didn't hear Leila and walked away in the middle of her sentence.

During science class, Leila tried to get Kait's attention with Kait's favorite thing: a note. But when Kait opened the note and saw who it was from, she crumpled it up. On the bus, Leila tried to sit next to Kait, but Kait had already taken the seat next to Javy.

When Leila got home, she immediately plopped on her bed and started talking to Nugget. "Errrrg, this is so frustrating!"

Nugget laid next to her and put his head on her lap.

"I mean, I finally figure out the second clue, but I would feel bad about going on until I make things right with Kait, you know?"

Nugget gave Leila's hand a little lick. He knew.

"I know I should have told her before; I just didn't want her to blab it to the whole school. But guess what? She somehow ended up blabbing anyways! So now, who knows if Kait will ever forgive me? And while I'm worrying about that, someone else might find the clue before I do! Should I just look for the clue now?

Do you think Kait would understand?"

Nugget rolled over for a tummy rub. Leila started scratching. Nugget wiggled around until he found a cozy spot, then lay there with his eyes closed and tongue half hanging out of his mouth. Leila sighed. "Yeah, I know."

Leila got a few things together, walked to Kait's house and knocked on the door. Kait's mom answered. "Hi, Leila!" Then she looked down at Nugget, puzzled. "What's this?"

"Hi, Mrs. Korver. It's a message for Kait. Can I talk to her?"

"Kait!" Mrs. Korver yelled. "Nugget has a message for you!"

"Can't come to the door!" Leila heard Kait yell from upstairs. "I'm busy!"

Mrs. Korver shook her head. "Hold on," she muttered to Leila as she turned around and walked upstairs. A minute later, she returned, holding Kait by the arm.

"What?!" Kait asked.

"Look." Her mom pointed.

Nugget was staring back at Kait with giant puppy eyes and a sign around his neck that said, "I'm sorry."

"So?" Kait asked.

"So you listen to her," Mrs. Korver said. "You don't ignore someone who's trying to apologize." Kait sighed, and her mom left.

"I'm sorry," Leila said.

"OK."

"No, I mean it. I had this secret, and I wanted it for myself. It felt special, ya know? But friends share stuff with each other, especially secrets. You're my best friend, Kait, and I should have shared this secret with you. I understand why you would feel hurt. Do you forgive me?"

Kait folded her arms across her chest. Nugget looked up and wagged his tail harder.

"Also," Leila added. "I think I figured out the riddle, and I was wondering if you'd help me look for the next clue."

Kait was trying to play it cool, but she

couldn't stop her eyes from lighting up. "You figured it out?"

Leila nodded. "But you didn't answer my question. Do you forgive me?"

"Of course I forgive you," Kait said. "You were probably right anyways. I mean, I do like to blab. Now tell me what the clue means!"

Leila smiled. "Well, first, we're going to have to go to Mrs. Crenshaw's house."

Kait made a face. Leila knew that Kait didn't like Mrs. Crenshaw because Mrs. Crenshaw had yelled at her a few years ago. "Unnnnnng," Kait said.

Ten minutes later, Leila, Kait and Nugget were walking to Mrs. Crenshaw's house. They would have left earlier, but Kait had insisted on finding her fastest running shoes in case Mrs. Crenshaw tried throwing her in a pot of boiling water and she needed to run away. When they reached the house, Mrs. Crenshaw opened the door and welcomed Kait by holding out her hand. "Hello there, I'm Mrs. Crenshaw."

Kait paused, then shook her hand. "Kait Korver," she said. "Uh, how do you do?" Kait wasn't normally the type of kid who goes around asking people, "How do you do," it just seemed like the right thing to say to people Mrs. Crenshaw's age based on Kait's experience with black-and-white movies.

"Korver, huh?" Mrs. Crenshaw said. "Hm, interesting."

"Interesting?" Kait asked, alarmed. "Why is that…"

"I think I figured out the clue!" Leila blurted. She'd been keeping this inside for far too long, and she couldn't bear to hold it in any longer. She walked to the kitchen and took off her jacket. As she walked, she kept talking. "What's black and white and red all over?"

"A newspaper," Mrs. Crenshaw and Kait answered at the same time. "It's the oldest joke in the world," Kait added.

"Right," Leila said. "It's a good joke to tell someone else, because 'read' and 'red' are easy to confuse when you hear them."

"OK," Kait said. "So?"

"Remember the clue? 'Columbus sailed the ocean BLUE. What would it mean if the sea were GREEN.' The two colors were capitalized in the poem. Then I realized the third capitalized word might also be a color." She pulled the Bobo Bar out of her pocket and pointed to the inside wrapper.

"Ohhhh," Kait said. "It's red!"

"Would it change the things you've READ!" Leila said. "This red wrapper is the key to figuring out the next clue!"

"I don't get it," Kait said.

"The poem makes it sound like the red color would change things. That made me think of those spy lens codes they sometimes have on cereal boxes. Do you know what I'm talking about?"

Kait shook her head.

"The back of the cereal box will have a jumble of shapes and numbers that don't look like anything. But if you cover the picture with the 'spy lens' you find inside of the box, you can see through the mess, and a secret code appears. Well, the spy lens is just a colored piece of plastic like the Bobo Bar wrapper. So if this is a spy lens code, we need to put the red wrapper over a map of the ocean that Christopher Columbus crossed!"

Mrs. Crenshaw started clapping. "That's brilliant!" she said.

"But what map?" Kait asked. "Any

map in the school from 70 years ago has to be gone by now, right?"

"Gone from the school," Mrs. Crenshaw said. "But maybe not gone altogether." She disappeared into the living room.

"See?" Leila said. "She doesn't bite."

"That's what she wants you to think while she figures out a way to kidnap us," Kait said.

Mrs. Crenshaw returned a minute later. "Put your jackets back on, girls. We're going to find this map."

Kait's eyes got wide. Leila laughed. "Come on, Kait, it's OK." Kait shook her head and backed up, ready to use her running shoes. Leila looked back at Mrs. Crenshaw. "Maybe it would help if you told us where we were going."

Mrs. Crenshaw smiled at Kait. "We're going to your grandmother's house."

8

THE ZOO

In the car, Mrs. Crenshaw explained why they were visiting Kait's grandma. "Kait, your grandmother and I have become quite close over the last few years because we both share the same interest — books."

Kait made a face at Leila in the back seat. Books were definitely *not* one of her interests.

"A few years ago in one of our book clubs, I mentioned a book I'd remembered from my childhood — *Happy Birthday, Mr. Tortoise*. It was the first pop-up book I'd ever seen, and I remember that it felt like magic. I spent hours as a child opening and closing the pages to figure out all the folds that made the pop-up pictures work. Well, the next week in book club, your grandmother gave me that exact book! It was 75 years old, and some of the pictures had been ripped, but your grandma had taped everything back together, so it was almost as good as new. She said she'd found the book in her attic. Kait, did you know your grandma was the school librarian for 40 years?"

"Mmhmm," Kait said. "It's all she ever wants to talk about."

"When the school got rid of old books, your grandma would get to take them home with her. She has quite a collection in the attic."

"Oh, I know," Kait said. "When I was little, my cousins and I would build huge forts up there with all the books until my grandma found out and made us stop."

"There's one book in particular that I asked her to look for. I hope she has it."

When they arrived, Kait's grandpa opened the door. "Pumpkin!" he said when he saw Kait.

"Poppy!" Kait gave him a hug. Then she noticed the old Scottish Terrier at her grandpa's feet. "Hey, Baxter!"

The dog gave her a little tail wag, then his eyes got big when he saw Nugget bound toward the door. Nugget ran up to the elderly dog and jumped around him for a full minute while Baxter waited patiently.

Kait's grandma came down the stairs holding the biggest book Leila had ever seen. "Hi, Kait, hi, Margie," she said. She gave Mrs. Crenshaw an air kiss on both cheeks. "I found the atlas you wanted."

"That book is humongopotamus!" Leila exclaimed.

Mrs. Crenshaw nodded. "I think it was the biggest book at the school for a long time, right Judy?"

"You're probably right," Mrs. Korver said. "I remember Principal McGee was so proud of it. It came from his personal collection."

Everyone gathered around the old book as Kait's grandma carefully opened it and started turning pages. Each page had a giant map of a country, complete with hand-drawn details and fancy lettering. Mrs. Crenshaw broke the silence. "I remember going to the library sometimes after school just to flip through this atlas and imagine traveling to the countries inside."

Kait made a face. "You read a book of maps?"

"Life was pretty exciting back then, huh?"

"There's something special about these kinds of books though," Mrs. Korver said. "It's too bad the school library can't buy them anymore. It just got too expensive, especially since students could find everything they needed online. Still, nothing's quite the same as getting lost in a big, old book like this."

They kept turning pages until they got to a full spread of the Atlantic Ocean. Leila got a tingling in her tummy as she pulled out the candy bar wrapper. "Let's see what we've got!" Everyone huddled around while Leila carefully slid the wrapper over the page. Nothing popped out.

"Try it again," Mrs. Crenshaw whispered.

Leila did. Nothing. She sighed. "Maybe it's on a different…"

"THERE!" Kait squealed.

Leila looked down. "I don't see anything."

"That dragon thing! Go back to that dragon thing!" Kait was so excited that she was jumping up and down.

Leila slid the wrapper back down to the corner of the page. There it was! Hidden in the tail of a big, red sea monster was a small set of numbers and letters written in green — 736.98. "Wow, Kait! You're a genius!"

Kait was grinning ear to ear. "A rich genius! We're getting $736.98!"

"That's not money, dear," Kait's grandma said. "It's a Dewey Decimal number."

Kait's grin turned into a frown. "Oh. Uh, what's that? Is it like money?"

Now it was Mrs. Korver's turn to frown. "The Dewey Decimal System? It's the number system used to organize books in the library."

Kait stared blankly at her grandma. "Oh."

Mrs. Korver groaned. "Where did I go wrong? In the Dewey Decimal System, the 700s are all books about art, and the 730s all have to do with sculpting. Now a book numbered 736.98 would be about..." Mrs. Korver looked at the ceiling for a moment. "Paper folding and origami."

Everyone stared at Mrs. Korver with their mouths hanging open. Even the dogs. "You just knew that?" Kait asked. "Off the top of your head?"

Mrs. Korver winked. "I was a librarian for a long time."

"So you think the next clue is in a book about origami?" Leila asked.

"There's only one way to find out!" Mrs. Korver said as she gleefully led everyone to the attic. Once they'd all reached the top of the creaky stairs, Mrs. Korver clicked on a single lightbulb. Leila gasped. It looked like every book that had ever been written was stuffed in the attic. Bookcases, shelves, bins, boxes — all overflowing with old books. "How will we ever find it?!" Leila asked.

"What kind of librarian would I be if I didn't sort this all by the Dewey Decimal System?" Mrs. Korver replied.

Sure enough, less than a minute later, they'd found the only origami book in the attic and started flipping through it. Kait used the Bobo Bar wrapper to look for another hidden clue. Leila searched for suspicious writing. Mrs. Korver inspected the check-out card. Nobody found anything until Mrs. Crenshaw made a suggestion.

"You don't think he used the bookmark secret, do you?"

Mrs. Korver's eyes lit up. "Kait, can you get a butter knife from the kitchen?"

"What's a bookmark secret?" Leila asked as Kait ran downstairs.

"When we were in school, the students had this little game where we would pass notes to each other by hiding bookmarks in the binding of big books. We all thought we'd kept it a secret from the adults, but Mr. McGee was smart.

He knew all of our tricks."

Kait returned with a butter knife, and Mrs. Korver carefully slid it down the spine of the book. "I think I hit something!" she said. Everyone leaned in as she pushed the knife farther and farther until a yellow piece of paper peeked out of the bottom.

"Eeeps!" Kait squeaked.

Mrs. Korver pulled the paper all the way out and held it up. It was a beautifully folded paper penguin with another Dewey Decimal number written on its wing. Kait squeaked again. "Where's this one?!" she asked.

"Should be a cookbook," Mrs. Korver replied.

Five minutes later, Mrs. Korver pulled a paper elephant from the spine of an old book called, *The Handy Cookery*. That elephant had another Dewey Decimal number on it that led them to a turtle in a history book, which led them to a snail in an astronomy book. Written on the snail was another poem. Mrs. Korver read it aloud for everyone.

You've completed your zoo,
Onto the final clue!
If you're brave and strong,
You won't be wrong —
Just climb up, up and away.

Mrs. Korver set the snail down and smiled at everyone. "I know where it is."

THE FINAL CLUE

Leila and Kait were the first ones off the bus when it pulled up to school the next day. "Let's go, let's go, let's go!" Kait yelled as she ran inside.

Leila shushed her. "Right now, we're the only ones who know about this. We've got to keep quiet to make sure nobody gets to the treasure before us. Got it?"

Kait nodded, made a lip-zipping motion and turned into the gymnasium. Leila followed her. Inside the gym, Leila pulled her dad's big binoculars out of her bookbag and started scanning the rafters.

"See anything?" Kait asked.

Leila shook her head. "Your grandma said it was in the middle of…"

"Hey!" A voice interrupted them. "You girls need to get to class!"

Leila gulped. It was Mr. Glaser, the P.E. teacher. Mr. Glaser was the scariest teacher in school. He wasn't exactly mean, but he did kind of act like he was running an Army boot camp most of the time in gym class. Plus, he used to be a football player, and even though that was a long time ago, he was still really big and muscley. Kait did the talking.

"Hi, Mr. Glaser," Kait said. "We're looking for the rope."

"The what?"

"The rope!" Kait repeated. "Ya know, the one that went all the way up to the ceiling."

Mrs. Korver had told the girls about a

big rope that used to be in the gymnasium. Students would have to climb all the way to the top for P.E. class. Both her and Mrs. Crenshaw agreed that it was the worst thing they ever had to do in school. "Strong and brave, climb up, up and away..." The clue must have been talking about the rope.

Mr. Glaser looked confused. "The school cut that down 20 years ago."

"We know. We're just trying to figure out where it was tied. Do you remember?"

"I wasn't even the P.E. teacher then."

"But you went to school here, right?" Kait asked. "Can you remember where it was when you were a kid?"

Mr. Glaser's patience was wearing thin. "Are you going to tell me what this is about?"

"A treasure," Kait said matter-offactly.

"OK, you two really need to get to class."

Kait crossed her arms. "And you really need to return The Secret of Wildcat Swamp."

Mr. Glaser squinted at her.

"Thaaaaat's right," Kait said. "The Secret of Wildcat Swamp. Hardy Boys Book #31. You checked it out from the school library on November 3, 1984, and you haven't returned it yet. Even if we go by the 1984 fine rate of five cents per day, you owe $620.50. You've been running from the law for a long time, mister, and my grandma sent me in to collect. Of course, she's willing to forget about the fine if you help us find the clue."

Mr. Glaser rolled his eyes. "What is it?" he asked — not so much because he was afraid of paying an old library fine, but because the girls didn't seem to be going anywhere until they got their answer. Leila explained the treasure hunt and the clue as fast as she could.

Mr. Glaser looked skeptical. "So you think there was some sort of treasure clue at the top of the climbing rope?" The girls nodded. "I've got to tell you," Mr. Glaser said, "I climbed up there a bunch of times when I was a kid, and I never saw anything."

"Can you just look?" Leila pleaded. "It would make us really happy."

"And it would make you happy to not have to pay a $600 library fine. Mwahahaha!" Kait added.

"I'll look up there," Mr. Glaser said. "But only because your grandma was always nice to me." Mr. Glaser disappeared into the equipment room and re-emerged a few seconds later pushing the Mover-Matic, an elevator platform he used to hang banners from the rafters and retrieve balls that had gotten stuck.

"See that hook thing up there?" he asked, pointing to the ceiling. "That's where the rope was." He locked the Mover-Matic into place and climbed onto the platform.

Kait's eyes got big. "Do you think…"

"Absolutely no kids allowed on the Mover-Matic!" Mr.

Glaser said as he pressed a button and started rising in the air.

"Worth a try," Kait whispered to Leila.

Once Mr. Glaser made it up to the hook, he took a few seconds to look around. "Definitely no clue," he finally said. "I'm coming back!"

"Wait!" Leila yelled. "Keep looking! What else is around the hook?"

"Six tons of steel beams," he said. "I'm coming down." The platform started moving back down.

But Mr. Glaser did a funny thing after he pressed the down button. He quickly ran his hand over the steel beam. Even though he said he didn't believe in the treasure, even though he was giving up, even though he acted like Leila and Kait were silly for making him do this, there still must have been a tiny part of him that wanted to believe something was up there.

"Whoa." Mr. Glaser said after he felt the beam. He stopped the platform.

"What is it?!" Leila yelled.

Instead of answering, Mr. Glaser moved the platform back up to get a better look. He got real close, then peeled something off the top of the beam. "I don't believe it!" he said. "It looks like a note!"

The girls jumped up and down and met Mr. Glaser when the Mover-Matic finally reached the floor. "Thank you! Thank you so much!" Leila said.

Mr. Glaser shook his head. "I wouldn't have believed it if I hadn't seen it with my own eyes," he said as he handed the yellowed piece of paper over to Leila. Leila carefully unfolded it and read it aloud.

Use your herd
To guess the magic word.
Then tell it to the man
Where it all began,
And the treasure will be yours!

The three of them were silent for a second. Finally, Kait asked, "What does it mean?"

"Yeah, what do you think it means?" a voice behind Kait repeated.

Oh no. Leila recognized the voice. It was Gwyneth Watson — the same girl who'd been trying to figure out the Bobo Bar clue the day before. She must have noticed Leila and Kait running off the bus and followed them to the gymnasium. With all the excitement of the final clue, Leila hadn't noticed her. Maybe she could convince Gwyneth to keep this little secret for just a bit longer.

Leila started to turn. "Hi, Gwyn…"

She froze. Behind Gwyneth, waiting eagerly for her response, was half the school.

PINECONES

And just like that, Leila's secret, little treasure hunt had become the opposite of secret and little. Anyone who hadn't seen the final clue with their own eyes had heard all about it within an hour. By lunchtime, the whole school was searching for treasure — even some of the teachers! And if that weren't bad enough, Channel 5 News had gotten wind of the 70-year-old treasure, and they came to the school with cameras and everything.

Leila felt sick. She walked Nugget around the block three times after school that day, fuming the whole time. "It's not fair!" she said to Nugget.

He responded by sniffing a tree.

"After all that hard work, now someone else is going to find my treasure."

Nugget picked up a pinecone with his mouth, looked back at Leila and tried to sprint ahead. He quickly dropped it, though, when he ran out of leash.

"Unnng. Do you think there's still a chance?"

Nugget picked the pinecone back up and zigzagged for the next few minutes to keep Leila from stealing it. Leila barely noticed. She'd made up her mind.

"I'm going to find that treasure first because I'm going to work harder than everyone else."

And she did work harder than everyone else. Leila thought about the

case every spare second of every day —
even some non-spare seconds while she
was supposed to be listening in class.
Every day, she had a new clue to add to
her notebook. Every afternoon, she had a
new idea to share with Nugget on their
walk. And every walk, Nugget had a new
pinecone to steal.

Leila quickly discovered that she had
two big problems. One was that she had
no idea what the "magic word" was. She
figured it must have something to do
with the origami animals because the clue
mentioned "the herd." But no matter
how long Leila spent staring at the
animals or how many times she unfolded
them, she couldn't figure out the magic
word. Then, there was the bigger
problem that "the man where it all
began" had been gone for 70 years. Even
if Leila did figure out the magic word,

she couldn't tell it to Mr. McGee. So what was the point?

The point was Leila had come this far, and she wasn't giving up now. So she kept looking and thinking and digging every day. Of course, she wasn't alone. The week following the discovery of the final clue was a full-blown treasure frenzy. Treasure clubs formed during lunch, hunting expeditions set out during recess and teachers even canceled some of their classes so students could look for the treasure together. Although Leila was worried about all the new people looking for the treasure, she took comfort in knowing that none of them had the origami collection. She swore Kait to secrecy — neither of them could breathe a word about the animals to anyone. It was their only hope of figuring out the final clue first.

She didn't need to worry, though. Nobody even got close to finding the treasure. Soon, Leila was the only one looking again. The idea of a treasure right beneath your feet is fun, but actually searching the school and puzzling over clues for hours on end? No thanks. Even Kait, who'd been so excited to strike it rich in the early days, got bored. Every time Leila started discussing possible clues with her, Kait would try to turn the conversation back to what they'd do with all the money. She'd start talking about buying a five-pound gummy bear, then she'd wonder how much real-life CIA spy equipment costs, then she'd start rambling about her dream treehouse until Leila would finally give up on the conversation and go home.

Weeks and months went by. Now

every time Leila passed the new school building, she got sad instead of excited. The beautiful windows in front and the giant playground in back were reminders that the clock was ticking on her treasure. The worst moment came during the last week of school. After turning in the final math test of the year, Leila plopped back in her seat, breathed a sigh of relief and looked out the window to daydream. That's when the sigh turned into a groan. Right next to Mrs. Pierce's third-grade classroom was parked a giant, yellow bulldozer.

That day after school, Leila hung her head during her whole walk with Nugget. "This is it," she said. "Summer vacation starts tomorrow, and then the treasure will be gone for good."

Leila sounded so sad that Nugget stopped sniffing long enough to come back and nuzzle her.

Leila smiled and bent over to pet him. "Thanks, little buddy."

Nugget let her scratch him for a few seconds before galloping off again.

"I just thought for sure I'd find it," Leila continued. "Like for sure, for sure. I never even cared if it was gold or money or anything. I just wanted to know what it was! That's the worst part. Now nobody will know what it is."

Just then, Nugget started sprinting. He'd found the pinecone tree. He grabbed the biggest one of the bunch, then ran ahead like normal. But this time, after just a few steps, he stopped. Instead of zigging and zagging and trying to keep the pinecone away from Leila, he turned around, walked back to her and set the pinecone at her feet.

"Awwww!" Leila put her hand over

her mouth. "That's the sweetest thing ever, Nugget! That was so nice of you to share!"

Nugget started wagging his tail. Leila picked up the pinecone and stared at it for a minute. Suddenly, she knew what she needed to do.

I PLEDGE ALLEGIANCE

"Attention!" Leila said when she stepped on the school bus the next day. "Attention, everyone!"

A few sleepy eyes looked her way.

"I want to invite everyone to join together and help me search for the Englewood Elementary treasure today! We are stronger together than we are apart! Together, I believe…"

"Leila," Miss Carol said without turning around. "Can you please sit down so I can start driving?"

"Oh, uh, of course," Leila said.

As soon as she could, Leila got Kait

and Gwyneth Watson to help her gather a group of kids together to share everything she knew about the treasure. She told them about President Harrison, the secret in the map — she even brought out the origami animals.

"Wait," Gwyneth said as she turned the paper turtle over in her hands. "You had these the whole time, and you didn't tell anyone?"

"I didn't either!" Kait said, proud of herself for not blabbing this big secret.

"I really wanted to be the one to find the treasure," Leila said. "But I realize now that I was just being silly. Every clue I found came because someone helped me. Mrs. Crenshaw, Kait, Mr. Glaser — even my dog! So now I'm sharing this with all of you and asking for your help. Would you guys help me figure out the magic word?"

Everyone was on board. Mrs. Pierce's third-grade class was supposed to have an end-of-the-year party that day, but most of the juice and donuts went untouched because the entire class was working on the case. By ten o'clock, they'd organized into a code-cracking unit. Kait was at the front of the class with the pointer, tapping animal names on the board. "Penguin, Elephant, Turtle, Snail. What do those four animals have in common? They all have four legs, obviously, so…"

"Penguins and snails don't," someone interrupted.

"They all have four legs, EXCEPT FOR PENGUINS AND SNAILS, I was going to say," Kait said. "So that's suspicious. Also, all four animals have been to outer space, I think."

Students looked at each other, confused. "What if the paper animals come to life when you put them in a certain spot in the school?" one of the kids suggested.

"Have you tried burning them?" someone else asked. "Maybe there'll be a clue in the smoke."

People started shouting half-baked ideas over each other until the room was complete craziness. Kait looked at Leila, threw up her hands and walked to her seat. Leila shook her head. It was a good try. She got up and walked toward the donut table. On her way, she passed Benjamin Balmer, the quietest kid in class. Without a word, Ben stood up, walked to the front of the classroom, picked up a piece of chalk and underlined the first letter of every animal — P̲enguin, E̲lephant, T̲urtle, S̲nail. Then he wrote the letters in order at the bottom of the chalkboard.

P-E-T-S.

Then he sat back down.

The room went silent. Leila stared with her mouth open. That had to be it. After all those months, she couldn't believe she hadn't thought to do that. "Uh, wow. Thank you, Ben. I think you just figured out the magic word," Leila said.

The room burst into applause.

Ben was a hero for about five minutes until everyone realized that they didn't know what to do with the code word. With Principal McGee gone, what good did it do? The class tried chanting, "Pets! Pets! Pets!" a few times, until Mrs. Pierce made them stop.

After she'd quieted everyone down, Mrs. Pierce spoke to the class. "I'm proud of you all for working together to solve this mystery," she said. "Although it didn't lead to an actual treasure chest, you all discovered the treasure of teamwork today, and that's worth all the gold in the world. Why don't you give yourselves a hand?"

The class halfheartedly clapped. The treasure of teamwork? Yuck.

Mrs. Pierce smiled and continued. "It's almost noon, so let's clean up and head to the flagpole for the Final Pledge. Then it's off to summer vacation!"

Leila sighed as she threw away her trash and took her place in line. For her, the treasure hunt was always more about figuring out the mystery than finding a bunch of gold. And they'd solved the mystery, right? So why wasn't she more excited? Kait patted her on the back. "You did great," she said.

When Mrs. Pierce's class walked outside and saw the scene at the flagpole, they all said, "Whoooooooooaaaaaa," at once. It looked like half the town was there. For as long as anyone could remember, it'd been Englewood Elementary's tradition for the students to gather on the last day of school for one final Pledge of Allegiance. With this being the last day for the old school, a bunch of extra people had joined the tradition this year. Parents, grandparents and people who'd graduated decades earlier had all come together to say goodbye to the old building. Mrs. Crenshaw was there, Kait's grandma was there, even the Channel 5 News crew had returned for the big occasion.

Principal Brown stepped in front of the crowd. "Wow," she said. "This is incredible. I know this place holds a special place in all of your hearts. As sad as we are to see it go, we are just as excited to make brand new memories in our new building this fall. Now, will you all join me as we salute the flag for one final Pledge of Allegiance."

Everyone put their hand over their heart and pledged as one.

"I pledge allegiance to the flag of the United States of America, and to the Republic, for which it stands…"

Kait looked around while she pledged. All the kids had giant grins on their faces as they tried to speed up the pledge so they could start summer break two seconds faster.

"…One nation, under God…"

A lot of the adults looked sad. One or two even had watery eyes. Leila could tell the moment was bringing them back to their childhoods, when this simple tradition marked the beginning of a three-month adventure away from school.

"…Indivisible…"

Wait a second. *Where it all began.* Leila's mind snapped back to the mystery, and her palms started sweating. She may have just figured out the whole thing.

"…With liberty and justice for all."

All the students cheered.

"Thank you so much!" Principal Brown said over the commotion. "Have a safe summer!"

As the crowd dispersed, the janitor, Mr. Peterman, walked to the flagpole to take down the flag. Leila quickly followed after him. "Excuse me, Mr. Peterman?" she said.

He turned around. "Yes?"

Leila's heart was beating out of her chest. "Pets."

Mr. Peterman stared at her for a second, then a big smile spread across his face. He walked to the platform that Principal Brown had been speaking from and got everyone's attention. "Excuse me!

Excuse me, everyone! I have one more announcement." He pulled Leila onto the platform with him and held up her arm. "This young lady just claimed a 70-year-old treasure!"

TREASURE WHEREVER YOU GO

One voice squealed above the noise of all the confused people.

"AHHHHH!"

It was Kait.

"AHHHHH! This is so exciting! AHHHHH!"

Kait pushed her way to the front of the crowd to hug Leila. "ARE YOU RICH NOW WHERE IS IT WHAT IS IT WHAT HAPPENED?!"

Leila smiled. "Seeing everyone here for the Pledge of Allegiance today made me think of a line from the last clue. 'Tell it to the man where it all began.' Remember?"

"Of course," Kait said. By this time, Kait's grandma and Mrs. Crenshaw had also made their way to Leila.

"We always thought that part was talking about Principal McGee because he was the one who began the treasure hunt. But that's not what the poem says. It says '*WHERE* it all began.' So it's talking about a place. And where was the treasure hunt supposed to have begun?"

"The flagpole!" Mrs. Crenshaw said.

"Exactly! So you're not supposed to tell the magic word to Mr. McGee, you're supposed to tell it to a man who will be at the flagpole. And since it's the last day of school, that man is going to be the one in charge of taking down the flag after the Pledge."

Mr. Peterman wiggled his eyebrows.

"Let me tell you all something that you're not going to believe," he said as he flipped through his keychain. "When you become the Englewood Elementary janitor, you get two things from the old janitor: a set of keys and instructions to unlock a cover at the bottom of the flagpole if — and only if — a student comes to you with the code word, 'Pets.' I always assumed that second part was a joke until that clue came out a few months ago."

"I can't believe you never told me!" Mrs. Crenshaw said.

"I'm sworn to secrecy, Aunt Margaret!" Mr. Peterman said. "It's the Janitor's Code! Anyways, all that time went by with nobody claiming the treasure, so I just figured that it would be lost forever. Now, I can't wait to see what it is!"

Mr. Peterman finally found the right key, knelt at the flagpole and wiped off some dirt to reveal a small lock. By this time, dozens of people had crowded around the scene, including one of the news cameras. "Do you want to do the honors?" Mr. Peterman asked Leila when he pushed the key into place.

Leila grinned and turned the key. She expected it to be hard to turn since the lock hadn't moved in 70 years, but it clicked right into place. Leila opened the cover, reached into the compartment and pulled out a musty burlap sack.

"How much gold?! How much gold?!" Kait asked, trying to get a better view over Leila's shoulder.

"It's not that heavy," Leila said.

"Even better! Paper money!" Kait exclaimed.

Leila reached into the sack, and

everyone leaned in closer. "It's... it's..." she grabbed a stack of something and pulled it out. "Baseball cards?"

"Baseball cards?!" Kait exclaimed. "BASEBALL CARDS?!"

"I mean, they're pretty old baseball cards, so that's cool," Leila said as she pulled out more packs.

"That's not a treasure!" Kait said.

Leila reached back into the bag. "Wait, there's a box in here too!" Everyone leaned forward again as Leila pulled it out. "Oh, cool!" Leila said when she saw what it was. "It's an old doll!"

The Channel 5 cameraman sighed and lowered his camera. Real treasure would have been so great for TV ratings.

"Looks like there's a note taped to the back of the doll," Mrs. Crenshaw pointed out.

Leila opened it up. "It's one last note

from Principal McGee!" she said.

The Channel 5 guy turned on his camera again.

Leila cleared her throat and read it aloud for the crowd.

You did it! You found the treasure!
Baseball cards for him and a doll for her.
Now keep discovering! Continue learning!
Be growing, stay yearning,
And you'll surely find treasures wherever you go.

"I don't get it," Kait said. "Does that mean there are like baseball cards and dolls all over the place?!"

Leila shrugged. "I don't know. The best part of this treasure hunt wasn't the stuff at the end; it was all the cool clues hidden in plain sight. Maybe that's what Principal McGee was trying to say — if you keep your eyes open, you'll start finding awesome stuff all around you. What do you think, Mrs. Crenshaw?"

"I think you've figured it out again, detective."

Kait slumped her shoulders. "That's cool, I guess. I just think a mountain of money would have been cooler."

"Don't give up on that money mountain just yet," Mr. Peterman interrupted. He was holding the baseball cards. "These are 1940 Play Ball cards. They're really rare, especially in perfect condition like this. This set had Ted Williams, Joe DiMaggio, Shoeless Joe Jackson — if you find a couple of the good cards in these packs, you're looking at a few thousand dollars easy!"

Kait gasped. "You are rich! I'm friends with a rich lady! What are you going to do with all the money?!"

Leila thought about it for a moment. "Well, I don't really feel like it's my money," she finally said. "It kind of seems like it belongs to you and your grandma and Mrs. Crenshaw and our whole class for helping me with the clues. I wish there were a way I could share it with everyone."

"What about candy?!" Kait said. "You could give candy to everyone! Or maybe buy us all a TV or a pony or…"

"Books!" Leila interrupted.

"What?"

"Books! That's it! That's exactly the type of treasure Principal McGee was talking about!" Leila said. "Our school library isn't what it used to be, but we can fill it back up with all kinds of cool books for kids! What do you think about that, Mrs. Korver?"

Kait's grandma squeezed Leila. "I

think that's wonderful, honey! Just wonderful!"

Kait looked up in the air. "Uggggh! Why do I have to be friends with such a nerd?!"

"Hey, I think we can keep a few dollars to buy something fun for us."

"Like what?"

Leila smiled and gave her own clue. "What's an animal that's chewy and gooey?"

"An animal that's chewy?" Kait gasped. "A gummy bear?!"

Leila started walking away.

Kait followed close behind. "A five-pound gummy bear?! Please tell me it's a five-pound gummy bear!"

AUTHORS' NOTE

Hope you had as much fun reading Leila and Nugget's adventure as we did writing it! We're hard at work on the next book right now. You can sign up to get a note when that book comes out, find pictures of the real Leila and Nugget and more at leilaandnugget.com.

If you liked this book, would you consider telling a friend or posting a short review on Amazon? We'd really appreciate the help!

Also, we'd love to hear from you! You can email us about anything at dustin@dustinbradybooks.com.

Thanks again for reading our book!

ABOUT THE AUTHORS

Deserae and Dustin Brady are the parents of Leila Brady (a baby) and Nugget Brady (a dog). They live in Cleveland, Ohio. They do not own a five-pound gummy bear, but would very much like to.

ABOUT THE ILLUSTRATOR

April Brady is a professional illustrator in Pensacola, Florida. Deserae and Dustin feel lucky to have such a talented doggy-drawer as a sister-in-law.

Made in the
USA
Middletown, DE